THE TREASURE KEEPER

by Anita Williams

Illustrated by
Lynn Elam-Jones

Edited By Dawn L. Watkins

Bob Jones University Press, Greenville, South Carolina 29614

Library of Congress Cataloging-in-Publication Data

Williams, Anita, 1926-
The treasure keeper / by Anita Williams ; illustrated by Lynn Elam-Jones ; edited by Dawn L. Watkins.
p. cm. — (Pennant)
Summary: In trying to find out how to grow big enough to work with his father and uncle at the Brazilian street market, Marcos finds himself and his goats in a grand adventure.
ISBN 0-89084-835-1
[1. Brazil—Fiction. 2. Goats—Fiction.] I. Elam-Jones, Lynn, 1948- ill. II. Watkins, Dawn L. III. Title. IV. Series.
PZ7.W65582Tr 1995
[Fic]—dc20 95-32151
CIP
AC

The Treasure Keeper

Edited by Debbie L. Parker

Greenville, South Carolina 29614

Printed in the United States of America

ISBN 0-89084-835-1

15 14 13 12 11 10 9 8 7 6 5 4 3 2 1

To Wally,

and our children,

Ronnie, Randy, and Cindy,

for the heart and adventure of Brazil

A.W.

To Jennifer and Wil,

who have always been my treasures

I Timothy 1:12-17

L. E-J.

Contents

Chapter 1

Red Tub Treasure

Marcos and his goats lived in Brazil, a country mostly warm, mostly green, but sometimes damp. Now the sun was splashing across the meadow. And Marcos was laughing at his silly pets.

The two goats, Sugar Bread and Baby, were poking each other with their little goat horns. They romped in a feathery patch of yellow and orange weeds.

Sugar Bread, brown and full of funny doings, could find trouble, just half-looking. Baby, her soft snow-white daughter, padded right behind Sugar Bread, eyeing, sniffing, and watching. Usually she followed Sugar Bread into the same trouble.

A giggle rippled the air. It came from Marcia, who sat fishing at the pond's edge. Marcia, who was Marcos's sister—two years older and two inches taller—thought goats did such silly and unnecessary things.

Even now Sugar Bread was wibble-wabbling about, making no sense whatever. Being full of apple cores, she behaved ever so perky. Suddenly she hurtled herself into the air. Her four feet came down running, kicking.

She landed with a hard thud. She rammed a jagged stump. Wood splinters splattered the air.

Marcos and Marcia laughed, Marcia's hair bobbing up and down with her joy. Marcos's face went red, and he slapped his knees, laughing. Then he heard creaky wagon wheels and oxen feet hard on the road.

A dirty truck roared by, whipping up dust.

"Farmers going to street market," Marcia said.

"When I get big, I'll sell oranges at the street market," Marcos declared. He was thinking about the big colorful market with its juicy oranges and chatty parrots and cackling chickens and flippy fish.

Marcia never knew what went on in her brother's head. She smiled and turned back to fishing.

"It's breakfast time," Marcos told the goats, meaning he was hungry too and hoping they would follow without dawdling. Sugar Bread pushed on ahead, but Baby pitter-pattered along beside Marcos.

The goats' shed was perched on a green hill across the meadow—down through a valley and again up to the hill. The shed smelled of peanut shells and turnip peels, of dry brown hay and soft manure. It was a perfect home for Sugar Bread and Baby.

Marcos looked down from the hill. The wind circled, waving the tall grasses. Fat oranges bulged on rows of green trees. Right now he could see Uncle Antonio's brown arm reaching. Uncle Antonio had such fine long arms he could twist loose any orange on the tree.

Poppa's yank was quick and able too. If Marcos were big like Poppa and Uncle Antonio, he could work in the orange orchards. He would sell oranges at the street market too.

He left the goats munching breakfast, and headed toward home. He ran, rock-jumping, skipping, and zigzagging. A breeze fanned him.

The sunny kitchen smelled good, like piping fresh buttery bread and burnt black coffee. Milk bubbled in a pan on the stove. Purple jelly just waited to be spooned. Momma was preparing Grand-momma's breakfast.

Momma poured the frothy milk into a metal teapot. Coffee, black as night, went into another such pot. She added a cup and a spoon, placing everything on a tray, with fruit.

Grandmomma looked fine in her bamboo chair, a yellow robe warming her shoulders. She was wide and her face wise with little hills and valleys and a few brown knots. She smiled at Marcos, then dumped milk and coffee into her cup.

Marcos washed his hands, combed his dark curly hair, then hopped up on a tall kitchen stool. A thick chunk of hard-crusted bread found Marcos's buttery knife sliding across it. Jelly, purple as a midnight moon, got piled onto that.

Probably Marcos was thinking out a dream when he asked it: "Just when will I be big enough to work at the street market?"

Poor dear Grandmomma couldn't see so well, but she was always bright. Right now she looked quite amazed. "Hmmm . . ." she mused, her words proper. "You must find the secret of growing big."

Marcos stared. Grandmomma screeched her chair, then hobbled to the window. Her fingers squiggled in among twisty green stems and vines and leaves. After three tries and three frowns, she brought out a little red tub.

Marcos bounced down from the stool, hurrying to see. Shooting upward from the tub through the moist black dirt was a skinny green stem with three sturdy leaves.

"It's a rubber tree from the hot country," Grandmomma said, her voice wrinkly and proud. "You may keep it. Give it lots of water and sunshine, and it will teach you much."

A smile swished Marcos's face. "Thank you, Grandmomma," he said, reaching. He ran full-speed toward the goats' shed, the little red tub tight against his chest.

Sugar Bread and Baby, no doubt, wondered about all this.

Marcos looked everywhere for the perfect spot. It needed to be sunshiny, warm, breezy enough, and safe from the goats who might chew on it. He found the spot—on the roof of Sugar Bread's shed!

The little red tub, round and damp, fit perfectly in its new spot of sunshine. It was far away from his other treasures—his pink ocean shell and his green growing sweet potato vine in the clear glass jar of water. But Marcos never minded that. Treasures did not need to be together, except on special occasions.

"Grow, rubber tree!" he commanded. "And I'll grow too!"

Chapter 2

Ornery Little Goat

The next day Sugar Bread's brown coat got an extraordinary wash job. The red soap Marcos slathered over her bubbled and foamed, snappy-crackly. He washed it off with slurping buckets of water from the pond.

"We're heading for town to sell Sugar Bread's milk," Marcos told Marcia.

"Good selling," Marcia wished him.

The little town was quaint, and its buffy houses gathered in close together. Squealing children played hide-and-seek and licked Popsicles. They stared at the boy and his goat.

Sugar Bread went sniffing, her feet bouncy on the dusty street. Marcos, his voice high and strong, yelled, "Milk! Fresh goat's milk!" People looked out from windows. They stopped their work to look.

"Just a minute, boy," a voice sang from a doorway. A lady with a metal bucket stepped into the street, her bucket swinging.

Marcos noticed Sugar Bread's mouth twitching.

He was thankful she stood still while he milked. The foamy milk bubbled up to the brim. A few drops sloshed over the sides of the bucket.

The lady bent to rub Sugar Bread's brown head. "Silky and soft," she said. She paid Marcos money. Then she drew out a sweet-smelling orange from her pocket. "Here, boy, something for you and the little goat."

Marcos said, "Thank you," and moved on down the street. A waggly cart went by, smelling like hot peanuts. Sugar Bread sniffed high, her nose wriggling. Two bicycles spun past, wheels shining silver.

Marcos's finger dug into the juicy, drippy orange. He stripped off a thick patch of peel and tossed it high into the warm air. "Catch it, Sugar Bread!" he commanded.

But looking around, he didn't see Sugar Bread at all.

He saw a lady carrying baskets on her head. A store man dragged a burlap bag of beans to a curb.

A child tugged at a rope of twisty candy. But Sugar Bread was not to be seen—anywhere.

A voice yelled. "Help! Help! Go away!"

A man sprinted down the street, Sugar Bread pounding hot behind him. The ornery little goat's head swung low. Her white horns aimed inches away from the man's skinny back. "Wheee!"

Marcos's sandals scattered the dust as he ran too.

A store man chased them with a broom. People were calling out from second story windows. Children giggled and pointed and jumped up and down. The Bread Man waved from his wagon.

Suddenly the man gave a flying leap through an open gate. With a wet, burning face he slammed the gate shut.

Sugar Bread tried to ram the man, but he had disappeared into a house. Her little feet bumped back and forth on the dirt street.

The man with the broom plopped down on the curb to watch. Servant girls stopped their work, and store customers came out to see.

Sugar Bread's eyes were rolling, her horns tucked low.

She butted the wooden gate. Then she walked up closer to the gate and reared up on her two hind legs. Grumbly, grouchy noises came out of her mouth, and her eyes spun around.

An enormous roll of laughter came from a fat lady leaning from a high window. "Funny little goat," she called down. "Funniest happening around here in a long time."

Her laughing started deep and soared high—high and loud. Other folks started laughing too.

People came out from the little corner market to see what was going on. Some leaned over big kegs of beans. They peeked around cheeses and sausages, peering out from the midst of yellow brooms.

Marcos felt embarrassed. He just wanted to go home. All he had to do was call. Sugar Bread clattered to her feet and trotted toward him.

"You bad, bad little goat," Marcos said.

But the laughing fat lady tossed an apple to Sugar Bread. It bounced to the ground, and Sugar Bread grabbed it with her mouth. The people laughed and began to scatter.

"Good show, little goat," she called down. "Do another one someday."

Feeling silly, Marcos picked up Sugar Bread's rope. The tattered thing had trailed along with Sugar Bread while she chased the poor man. Marcos and his goat headed back the other way, toward home.

They went past the town and over grassy meadows. Fat clouds chugged through the sky.

Marcos began whistling. But mostly he was thinking. Uncle Antonio drank Sugar Bread's milk, and he was big and brown. Poppa drank Sugar Bread's milk, and he was tall and strong. Marcia was tall and pretty. Grandmomma was very wide. Even Momma was plump and nice.

What he wondered was, why was he, Marcos, so short? And he was skinny too.

At home he and Sugar Bread found Baby munching grass in the big field. "Time for your lunch too, Sugar Bread." He left the two chewing on the tall grasses.

Then he ran, all the way, not stopping to look right, or left, or even to fix his sandal that kept sliding.

At the shed, broken peanut shells crunched under his step. Turnip pieces squished. He shinnied up to the rooftop.

When Marcos saw the wondrous rubber tree, he grabbed a sunshiny-hot breath.

Three silvery green leaves actually glowed in the sun that fell across them. The rubber tree was true! He gave it fresh water. He loosened the black dirt with his fingers.

It would grow. He would grow. He wriggled to the ground, whistling, running. He pushed hard into the wind, letting it wash his face with coolness. He barely touched the ground.

Chapter 3

Eyes in the Dark

The next morning Marcos saw a red bird. He chased a yellow butterfly all the way to the goats' shed. Sugar Bread and Baby gulped two buckets of water while he put down fresh turnip peels.

When he thought of what he'd been thinking, his brown eyes looked around and around. His look went past the long green meadow, past the tall weeds. On the other side of that cluster of floppy trees, there was a cave—a dark and scary cave.

Nobody ever went inside the cave. Nobody ever came out. But something must go on in there. He would explore the dark cave! He shot off, like a fast bird, eyes hard on the opening of the cave.

The meadow stretched long, green and brown. A fence ran alongside a neighbor's farm. Marcos jumped a ditch, landing squarely in front of the big black hole.

Dirt and vines and great brown boulders covered its top. The hole was round and deep and black, with no stopping of its darkness.

"Marcos!"

Marcia was half-running, half-skipping toward him, shiny curls bouncing.

She hardly had breath when she asked, "You're going to explore the cave, aren't you?" Her dancing eyes studied the dark hole. "You shouldn't go in there alone."

Marcos and his sister peeked inside, stooping, bending, and pushing their heads just a bit into the cave's blackness.

"We can see a part," Marcos announced. What he saw were more rocks, more dirt—the dirt looked damp and messy.

When Marcia said, "We won't go in very far," the two wriggled inside, Marcos first. Their sandals squished in the soft, wet ground, making prints.

In the dim light they saw long curls of rock growing down. Wavy rocks rose to the cave's top. The rocky pathway slid deeper. Dark went darker to sooty black.

When their walkway flopped into a blind hole, Marcia, in a tiny scared voice, said, "I think we shouldn't go one step more."

But Marcos was hearing sounds, like slurping, or guzzling. "Shhh!" he said.

Something swirled. It gurgled and splashed.

"It's a river!" Marcos was sure of it. "A little river inside the cave."

"Don't m-move!" Marcia said. "We could s-slip into that r-river."

"What," Marcos wanted to know, "would happen if we fell in?"

"We would wash away," Marcia said. "Over bumps and rocks." They were quiet a moment. "Right on out to the ocean," Marcia said, forgetting to be scared for a moment while she thought of their journey down the river. "Maybe the fish would eat us up too."

Marcos dug his toe into the cool damp dirt. The noisy little river seemed to be chuckling at them. It sounded friendly to him, and laughing because they were there.

Just then Marcia grabbed at his shirt. "Marcos, wh-what's that?"

"What?"

"Eyes! See those eyes!"

The eyes, looking right at them, sparkled and shone in the darkness. Did the eyes stare at them from this side of the river, or from the other side? Marcos couldn't tell. Maybe the eyes came up out of the river.

"I think, I think we should get out of here," Marcos stammered.

"Me too!" And already Marcia was inching toward the round cave door.

They couldn't run, and they couldn't walk fast either. The top was low and the floor rocky and the walls tight as clothes pins. So they stumbled, falling sometimes, over the steep rocky path.

Behind them was darkness, but that didn't keep them from looking back. And every time The Eyes were staring at them.

"Hurry!" Marcos urged.

"Ouch!" Marcia's yell was so loud that Marcos fell back, almost sliding down into the river.

"Oh, my foot!" she sobbed, forgetting to talk softly so The Eyes wouldn't notice her. She sat down on the rocks of the cave, crying a little and rubbing her foot.

"You'll have to limp," Marcos said. He kept worrying about The Eyes, turning to see if they had moved. The Eyes gazed out at them, but they hadn't moved.

He bent to help Marcia, and he saw a shine on the cave's dirt floor. The shine was round and solid. It looked like eyes, but it wasn't eyes. It was not large, but in the cool darkness it glowed.

Marcos whistled. He picked up a fancy rock, so clear it looked to be ice.

He held up the rock, seeing its shimmer and feeling its smoothness. He forgot about Marcia's hurting foot. He kept studying the wiggly white lines racing through the ice rock.

Marcos whistled.

"Marcos!" Marcia said. "Hurry!" She went on without him.

Marcos smiled at the ice eye in his hand. He would not run now. He dropped the ice rock into his pants pocket. He helped Marcia to the cave door. They squiggled out into the bright sunlight.

"Goodbye, Eyes," Marcia called back.

"Goodbye, Mr. Staring Eyes," Marcos yelled.

Chapter 4

The Bottle Man

On a sweet-smelling warm morning, with butterflies sailing and bumblebees buzzing, Marcos heard horses' feet. "Hey!" a loud voice roared, and Marcos recognized the Bottle Man.

Mr. Bottle Man collected bottles, rags, cans, lids, and old newspapers. He stuffed them in his big wooden wagon, pulled by two pokey mules.

"Bottle Man! Newspapers! Rags! Bottles for the Bottle Man!" His inviting call thundered out to the streets. Marcos liked to listen.

The Bottle Man never missed anything. He could spot a shine or a color or a shape anytime. Marcos's ice rock needed inspecting. Mr. Bottle Man would fit the job, a perfect rock inspector.

Marcos's eyes roamed the grassy yard. Almost at once he saw a tattered greasy rag, fine for Mr. Bottle Man's creaky wagon.

He scooped it up with one hand and hurried to the street.

The Bottle Man saw Marcos's rag hoisted in the air. He yanked his mules to a stop. "Thank you, boy," he said, his round red face smiling. He stuffed the rag in among blue bottles, yellow bottles, brown bottles, and crumpled old newspapers.

Suddenly the ice rock came up in Marcos's outstretched hand. "Look, Mr. Bottle Man!"

The Bottle Man's alert eyes rounded to big brown marbles. "Why, what have you here, little friend?"

Puffing, he reached down over his ample stomach to collect the ice rock Marcos held toward him. He flipped it over and over, fingers on its sharp edges. His eyes grew bigger and more curious.

Grinning, Marcos admitted, "I found it in the cave. It's white as ice with fancy wiggly lines."

"Hmmm . . . it's certainly different," the Bottle Man said, "and beautiful." He handed it back to Marcos. "But," he said, "I find bright and unusual things in my work all the time." He yelled at his mules, and the wagon started on.

"Wait!" Marcos begged. "Wait, Mr. Bottle Man. Show me the things you find."

The Bottle Man's face turned orange. He shouted at his mules to stop. "Okay, little friend. Come aboard!"

Marcos shinnied up to the wagon seat.

The wagon wheels sang with every turn. Cottony clouds played across the sky. A yellow wasp landed squarely on top of Mr. Bottle Man's hat.

Then the noisy wagon hushed to a stop.

"Now watch, boy." The Bottle Man's eyes squenched in the bright morning light. "In no time you'll see bottles and papers and rags. We want all of them."

Ever so carefully, Marcos watched.

He bounced to the road to pick up things for the Bottle Man. There were brown bottles, white bottles, and rags. The wagon stopped again and again, every minute or so. Twice he found some rumpled newspapers and even a ragged shoe.

They rolled through the town, past the market with sausages and pans and swinging brooms. Marcos's seat was high and important. Children shouted to him. An old woman waved her cane. He saw a cocky green parrot.

The Bottle Man's wagon whittled off a corner. Blocks of cozy houses disappeared. The wagon's wheels popped and groaned past fenced fields and green meadows.

By now the wagon was full—with rags, dirty bottles, and even colored buttons. The sun was hot and the road dusty and long.

The mules poked along. They dallied, their tired feet barely moving. Then they stopped.

"Go! Go!" the Bottle Man commanded. His face was hot, his stomach heaving.

The mules stood there, a fly buzzing at their ears. The Bottle Man shouted and scolded, and even shook his fist.

But the mules wouldn't move, not even an inch.

The Bottle Man's arms began swinging. "Get going, ornery mules!"

Marcos listened, thinking. Even mules had feelings. The poor worn animals were tired of trotting down country roads. Their feet burned from clop-clopping over pebbles and stones.

They didn't wish to go. So they didn't.

Mr. Bottle Man's face was hot and red and wet. His middle heaved up and down while he caught warm breaths.

Marcos thought about Sugar Bread. What made her get going when she didn't want to? He thought back, remembering, imagining. "Hey, Mr. Bottle Man!" he said. "I know how to outdo a mule."

Marcos bounced down to the ground. With his fingers he tickled the mules' ears. "Go, mules," he said. "When you get home, you'll find water and fresh hay."

But the silly mules paid no attention. They stood like statues. A blue fly buzzed. A flappy breeze fanned them. And they didn't move.

"Wait, Mr. Bottle Man!" Marcos made a long jump across a ditch, then squeezed under the wire fence. His quick eyes searched the ground till he found a cluster of fuzzy weeds.

Now what would those mules do?

Marcos stood, wriggling the funny fuzzy weeds under the mules' noses. The yellow brown weeds were not only fuzzy, they were itchy. Besides that, they were tickly and tingly and even a little bit sneezy.

The mules jerked. Their pink noses twitched. Ripples went across their brown backs. Their feet started kicking at the dusty road. And then they started walking.

Marcos hopped up on the moving wagon. The Bottle Man was having to hold his stomach, he was laughing so hard. "What a grand idea, little friend. You were smart, much smarter than my mules."

In the sun, Marcos's gate shone yellow. The heavy wagon clanked to a stop exactly in front. The Bottle Man said, "You've been good company, boy. You know how to outdo a mule."

He grinned. "So," he said, "you deserve a nice gift." He reached down to his left foot, drawing up a bottle Marcos hadn't seen. The bottle was strange, blue with green squares that had diamonds in them.

The sound of wagon wheels faded. Marcos stood, gazing down at the strange bottle. Its shine caught the blue of the sky and the green of the grass. Its diamonds shone like stars.

Suddenly Marcos threw back his head, laughing. Put this treasure with his other treasures, and he'd turn into a giant!

Chapter 5

The Flower Lady's Gift

The morning was so blue and full of sun that Marcos just had to scoot upon the gate. Besides, there came the Flower Lady, her basket resting upon her head. He liked her happy little step and flowing black hair. Her warm smile caught him up in it.

"Good morning, little friend." She lowered the brown basket, overflowing as it was, down to where he could see.

There were patches of red blooms and bluebells. Feathery yellows blossomed out like fans. Purples glowed rich and deep.

But he certainly didn't expect the Flower Lady to suggest what she did. "Want to come along and help me sell flowers?"

"Sure," Marcos said, jumping to the sidewalk.

The Flower Lady hoisted the basket of flowers to her head, and they started toward town.

Marcos hopped on one foot, then the other, around the walk's broken pieces. A red-headed bird whipped in so close that Marcos chased it.

Two creaking wagons clattered past. The milkman's stomping mules left holes in the dust. A servant girl stopped her sweeping to let them by.

"Flowers! Beautiful flowers!" the Flower Lady called out in her musical voice.

"Flowers! Beautiful flowers!" Marcos yelled.

People came out to admire the fresh, sparkling flowers. The Flower Lady let them choose. She said, "Thank you, ma'am," or "Thank you, sir," and folded the money into the pocket of her crinkly orange dress.

Marcos thought this to be fine work until they came to the next stop. There—tall and black—stood the iron fence he didn't like. It had skinny round bars and ugly ornaments. The black iron fence might be hiding something.

But, Marcos noticed, the Flower Lady wasn't afraid, so he wouldn't be scared either. Her small brown shoes marched right up to the big iron gate that had been swung open.

Marcos, with a jumpy look to the right, another to the left, padded behind her. From that spot, where the flappy green bush grew, he could see inside. Nothing was in there. Nothing but a winding road and waving palm trees and plants with big green fingers.

The Flower Lady touched her basket, smiling. She clapped at the gate, just like at the gates of little houses. They could see a garden man who wore blue clothes. He was kneeling, holding giant scissors.

"Come on up," he called, motioning.

Something growled. The gruffy noise came from behind a thick leafy bush.

Marcos's hand shot out to warn the Flower Lady. Then the Something hissed and snarled.

Marcos jumped.

"Oh, dear," the Flower Lady cried out. "What was that?"

Marcos didn't answer, for just then Something pounced at them. Marcos's heart flip-flopped.

The Something had ears pointed up straight like arrows. His eyes blinked open and shut, brown, then red.

And all the time he was making ugly, angry growls deep in his scrubby red throat.

The fearsome dog, catching hot breaths, rushed toward the Flower Lady. He aimed to snatch the basket of flowers from her head.

"Get!" the garden man shouted from the top of the hill. "Get out of there!"

Marcos couldn't think of what to do, not at first. He wished for Sugar Bread. That spunky little goat would poke the mean dog with her horns. She'd jump high, come down running, and her horns would ram the rascally dog.

Ideas spun about in his head. Why couldn't a boy pretend to be a goat? He could perform some of Sugar Bread's acts, couldn't he? Yes, he was sure he could.

He jumped up and down, back and forth, bending, tipping forward to his toes, landing back to his heels. His hands bounced to his head, fingers pointing like horns.

Strange noises sputtered from his mouth—throaty, grumbly goat growls. Then Marcos thrust his head down. He ran toward the dog. That's what Sugar Bread would have done. Exactly.

The monster dog's tail stiffened. He stopped growling. He stared at Marcos. Crazy, probably he was thinking. Crazy boy! Crazy as a goat!

The silly dog's ears flopped down. His slobbery mouth shook a little, but no sound came out of it. In another moment his long tail swooped down beneath his skinny hind legs. He stalked away, knowing he had lost that battle.

The Flower Lady giggled. Marcos caught his breath.

The garden man, seeing everything, hurried toward them, his big scissors swinging. "What a show!"

"Please sell me a bouquet for my wife," he begged. He used his own scissors to snip the wrinkly pinks and dark purples and cottony whites. Then the Flower Lady put them together in a soft bundle.

Marcos and the Flower Lady stepped out to the white walk, moving on past the ugly black fence.

"You were very smart," the Flower Lady said to Marcos on the way home. "You took the mean dog's attention away from my basket of flowers. You made him watch you instead."

Smiling, she added, "For that, Marcos, I want to give you a wonderful gift."

Her long brown fingers sifted through the greenery. He watched her draw out a moist flower of gold.

"It's a golden orchid." She was watching his face. "Very special and hard to find."

Marcos took the damp little flower into his hand. He'd heard wonderful tales of the search for the golden orchid up near the Big River. Its delicate gold held the yellow sunshine and the green forest.

For no reason that he knew, Marcos said to the smiling Flower Lady, "Someday I want to grow big so I can work at the street market."

The Flower Lady didn't laugh. Instead, her blue eyes looked very kind. They were gazing at the orchid's soft petals when she spoke.

"That is good, my little friend. Everyone must have his dreams."

The Flower Lady left Marcos at his own gate. Marcos called out "thank you" as she stepped away down the long sidewalk. In his hand he held his small damp treasure.

Certainly, it was the sunniest of all his wonderful treasures!

Chapter 6

A Coin for Keeping

The wondrous rubber tree kept growing higher, its leaves shinier. What it needed, Marcos figured, was a heavy pot, one for holding its spreading roots. On a morning while he was fishing, he wished out loud.

"If only I could think of some way to earn some money."

Marcia, who was fishing too, asked, "For what?"

"Something."

Grandmomma said the rubber tree grew in the hot country. It had sturdy leaves and strong roots. A rubber tree needed black moist dirt, thick in a heavy pot.

Marcos stood, letting his feet squiggle into the soft mud. Down, down, they went, oozy mud pushing through his toes till his bare feet couldn't be seen.

Now he had on shoes—brown oozy mud shoes. The cool wet mud squished around and over his toes and up to his ankle bones.

Slowly he drew out one drippy foot, then the second drippy foot. Mud shoes were heavy. They were cool. With his knee bent, he pulled one foot high. Down that foot sank, deep, then up came the other foot, high, knee bent.

Marcia giggled. "You're wearing mud shoes!"

Marcos high-stepped away. His drippy mud shoes pulled heavy. He was a high-stepping giant!

In the middle of a messy puddle he stopped. Sloshy mud shoes—what an idea! He could polish shoes at the city market, couldn't he? Of course he could. It was not so big as the street market, nor so important. People might pay money, and he'd use the money to buy a heavy pot.

Uncle Antonio, when he heard, told him, "That's a whistling good idea." Grandmomma smiled, and Momma helped him get things together.

The very next morning Marcos rode to town with the friendly Bread Man. When the wide doors of the city market opened, Marcos was there, carrying brush, rags, and polish.

The city market smelled like gritty potatoes and sweet syrup and dusty black beans and strong onions. People sold baskets and clothes and brooms and pans. Men yelled, "Oranges!" and "Tomatoes!"

So Marcos shouted, "Polish your shoes!" He sounded strong and able and worth noticing.

A tall man came over, smiling, pointing. "Sure, boy, go ahead."

Marcos reached for a clean cloth. First, he swished off the dirt. Then very evenly, he spread on black polish. With strong hands he rubbed, smoothing too.

With another cloth he polished, rubbing harder, harder. The man's black shoes glistened. The soft brush in Marcos's hands went like a broom. The man's shoes were new again.

"Good job," the man said. He handed Marcos a long yellow strip of gum.

"Thank you, sir," Marcos said, popping the juicy sweet gum into his dry mouth. He liked its fruity sweetness. But a strip of gum wasn't money. He needed money, so he yelled again, "Polish shoes!"

A round jolly man appeared, his flushed face damp. The shoe he stuck out was short and brown. "Fix up my shoes, son."

Marcos, smiling, worked with energy. Dirt flew, brown polish zipped over the shoes, which then got patted and rubbed and brushed. He hoped the man wouldn't pay him in gum.

The minute Marcos quit, the round jolly man unrolled his fingers. In his palm lay four bright balloons, one red, one blue, one yellow, and one green.

The man's mouth spread wide. "I knew you'd like these."

Marcos reached for the balloons, letting them slide, one at a time, into his pocket. "Thanks," he said again and watched the brown shoes walk away, gleaming.

The sun was a flashy ball in the morning sky. Folks stirred through the city market. Marcos had polished lots of shoes, but he hadn't earned any money. He had the four balloons, and one man paid him with three marbles. And there was a green melon which Grandmomma would like.

The hot sun burned the sidewalk, searing into the bottoms of his sandals. His knees were scratched from the rough sidewalk. Besides that, his gum had lost its fruity sweetness.

He started to go when a dark pudgy man stopped him. "Do a good job on my shoes, son. I'll pay."

Money probably, Marcos figured.

Marcos pretended he wasn't tired. He grabbed the rag, whisking away every speck of dirt. He patted on polish. He rubbed and brushed and shined. The man was so pleased he whistled.

His black shoes shone like a new mirror.

Smiling, he opened wide his hand. In it, looking quite small but most important, lay an old coin. In the bright light it appeared muddy and dark.

"It's very old and different." He watched Marcos's face. "The longer you keep it, the more valuable it will become."

"Yes sir," Marcos agreed, studying the fine old coin.

His customer, still whistling, disappeared into the city market. Marcos held the coin. He studied its silvery designs. The coin was round, its edges ragged and nicked.

Marcos let the old coin slide into a different pocket, separate from his wad of balloons and marbles. He wouldn't spend his coin—not for a very long time.

He gathered up his polishing stuff and the green melon.

All the way home he could feel that rich old coin in his pocket. And Marcos kept whistling.

Chapter 7

A Day of Happenings

Marcos rolled over so fast that he flopped out of bed onto the wood floor. White bars of sunshine fell across his room. Even the birds were telling him to get up.

He scrambled into long brown pants and a white shirt. It was the First of January, his birthday. It was the First of January, a big holiday in Brazil. There would be fireworks and feast food and parades with music. There might be dancing clowns.

Bands would march by, drums pounding, horns tooting. Marcos's foot started tapping. Fancy horses would high-step. Noisy firecrackers would crack and sizzle and boom.

He smiled from inside out. There would be a party too—his birthday party! Likely a cake would shine on the dining table, on it twinkly candles.

That's when Poppa and everybody else would see his wonderful treasures! When party time came, he'd bring them out, one at a time, proudly.

He bounced up to peek at Mr. Sweet Potato, a gift from the Vegetable Man. Mr. Sweet Potato's twisty vines looked nice in their water jar. The old coin had gotten its share of shining, being silver now. Grand-momma kept the golden orchid, and the ice rock had gone into poor Mr. Beggar Man's hand. But the blue-green bottle was there, its diamonds shining.

And there was always the wavy pink shell. Uncle Antonio had brought him the pink shell from the beach. Inside it, the ocean roared and crashed and smashed upon the sandy beach.

Probably the wondrous rubber tree was the best of his treasures. Its house, the little red tub, seemed quite proud too.

Dots of delicious smells seeped under his door. One was sizzling beef. One was fluffy rice. One was a syrupy brown pudding. But one smelled like a cake!

Marcos didn't stop by the kitchen but hurried to lead the goats to the pond.

He ran fast, and faster, Sugar Bread and Baby loping along beside him. This was feast day. It was parade day—and music and firecracker day. And his birthday!

When he returned, Momma was stirring syrupy sauce over the fire. Grandmomma sat wide in her bamboo chair, smiling.

Uncle Antonio nibbled on a hunk of yellow cheese. "Hi, Shorty. It's your day, isn't it?"

Probably it was the first time ever Marcos didn't mind being called 'Shorty.' He didn't care because it was his birthday. He would show his fine treasures. After that he would grow plenty.

"Marcos, go to the orchards to get Poppa. Antonio, find Marcia. Our holiday meal is almost ready."

Marcos found Poppa stacking oranges in a box.

"I'll be right there," Poppa said.

Marcos bubbled with so much energy he couldn't stand still. He zigzagged through the onions, high-jumping the cabbages. He even surprised the goats by walking backward.

"Feast day!" he yelled. He crossed the meadow, jumping logs and smashing through tall grass.

He circled the pond and bounced over gruffy weeds.

"Marcos," his mother called when he hopped the steps of the porch, "wash your hands."

Marcos whistled.

The dining room sparkled, little lights flickering. A round cake, frosty white and trimmed with red bells, rested in the middle. Blue candles burned, waiting for him to make a wish.

Poppa, strong and brown, sat at the head of the table, Momma next. Grandmomma's special chair was pulled close. Uncle Antonio and Marcia smiled at him. Marcos slid onto his own chair.

Everybody sang "Happy Birthday." Marcos made his wish, and with one poof blew out the candles.

"After we've had our holiday dinner, we'll cut the cake," Momma announced. Marcos smiled inside himself. That's when he'd bring out all his special treasures.

Peppery beef and hot tomatoes got piled on Marcos's plate. Yellow yams and rice too. Marcos's buttery knife slid into the middle of a hot chunk of bread.

For a while nobody talked.

Marcos was almost ready for a piece of cake. Then he heard music. He heard a drum's heavy roll. He heard the slam-bang noise of cymbals. There were feet walking and horns tooting. The parade was coming!

Momma was smiling at him. Marcia's face was glowing. Marcos forgot to be excused. Marcia's sandals clattered along behind him.

"They're having a parade because it's my birthday," Marcos said on the way out.

"Oh silly, not for just your birthday," Marcia said. She laughed. "It's because it's the First of January."

Just the same, Marcos liked to think part of the celebrating was for his birthday.

Marcos and his sister climbed up on the gate. Their feet tapped time with the music. They clapped for the silly clowns.

Clowns danced along, and smart brown horses high-stepped. Marcos and Marcia caught pink and yellow streamers in their hands.

After a while Marcia eased down from the gate, frowning. "My head hurts," she said.

"Too much drumming," Marcos said. "Too much horn-tooting." He went inside with Marcia.

He watched as Momma fed Marcia a spoonful of black medicine from the big bottle. After that Marcia went to sleep, with Momma saying, "When she wakens, she'll be fine."

Dusky night settled and Marcia didn't come out. Momma's face was pale, and she started to cry. Poppa left the house in a terrible hurry. Grandmomma wouldn't smile.

Nobody talked to Marcos.

In his room Marcos sat on the floor, staring at his treasures. The wondrous rubber tree looked lonesome and its leaves droopy. The blue-green bottle was plain, maybe ugly. Even Mr. Sweet Potato looked dark and angry. As for the silver coin, it was old and scarred.

He shuffled over to pick up the pink shell. It felt rough and hard, but he put it to his ear, listening, hoping.

He heard Mr. Ocean. The waves roared, but they didn't sound friendly. He heard the waves crashing against the white sand. They weren't playmates now.

Chapter 8

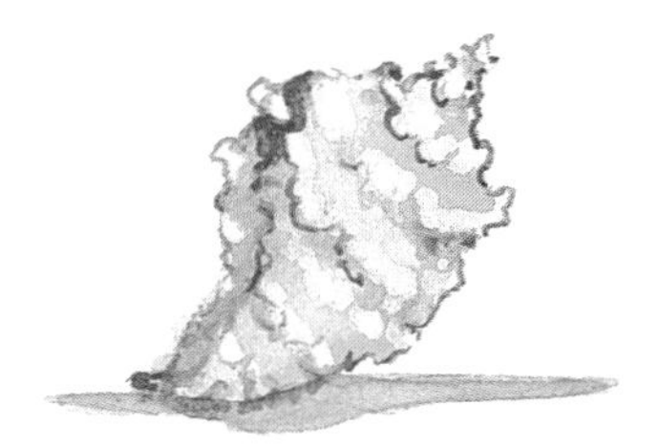

Something Special and Shiny

No laughing sounded in Marcos's house. No sweet yam or coconut pudding smells drifted from the kitchen. Shades were pulled so that morning sunshine did not come in.

Marcos saw the silent tears washing down Momma's cheeks. Grandmomma was hunched in her chair, head bowed, praying. Poppa didn't go to work. Instead, he tiptoed through the house, looking solemn.

Grandmomma whispered, "Shhh! You must be quiet. Marcia is very sick. We have to walk softly and whisper so she can rest."

Marcos stood behind the door as the doctor came inside. The doctor was short, with a black mustache and a small round belly. He carried a black leather bag, and he wasn't smiling.

The bag was full of strange tubes and bottles and long needles, Marcos imagined.

When the doctor stepped out from Marcia's room, he wore a scowl. He took Momma to the side and said something in a deep gravelly voice.

Marcos stared at the wall. Marcia might look crumply and wrinkly, maybe black.

He crept back to his room, making not a speck of noise. Something would make Marcia well, and he had to find it.

His eyes jumped about the room, taking in the green things, yellow things, twisty things, round things, and shiny things.

A breeze stirred the rubber tree's leaves. Mr. Sweet Potato's twisty vines twined down into the clear glass jar. Things alive and things shiny and things fresh—that's what girls liked.

Flowers! Of course, girls liked flowers. Marcia's eyes would smile when she saw a flower dipped in sunshine and wet with morning dew. The golden orchid—Marcia would love it.

Marcos bit his lip, remembering. Grandmomma kept the golden orchid folded in her handkerchief.

And the trouble was, it wasn't gold anymore, but shredded and mostly brown and mostly dry. It was like Marcia—crumply and wilted and broken.

Marcos's eyes rolled, then stopped. There—green as the meadow and shivery as the wet pond, stood the little rubber tree, shining. A sick girl needed to look at something alive—and growing and flappy green.

Nobody saw Marcos slip into Marcia's room.

Marcia's soft eyelashes fanned out from closed eyes. A yellow bedspread stretched over her. Her face was pale, but she wasn't black. Hearing him, she squeezed open an eye. Then the other eye flipped open. She saw the rubber tree in its little red tub. Her mouth made a tiny smile.

That evening Marcos heard Momma wonder aloud, "Why, where did the beautiful plant come from?"

The very next day Marcos marched right into Marcia's room. He didn't tiptoe either but stepped straight, eyes bright, grinning. Marcia, her face pink and a little pale, smiled back at him.

When she said, "Thank you," in that piping little voice, Marcos laughed. That almost made Marcia giggle. "For the green plant," she murmured.

"It's a sunshiny rubber tree," Marcos told her. "It came from the hot country. It's growing like a giant."

Marcia's smile made Marcos so happy he decided to run to the pond and back. Warm raindrops splashed on his curly head of hair. They slapped at the backs of his legs and patted his shoulders.

He wished Marcia were there, sliding on the slippery grass, laughing and free. The tingly air would waken her and put pink rounds to her cheeks. Whispering breezes might even put a dance in her feet.

Marcos jumped over a knobby log. Marcia wouldn't be able to sing and hop about again unless something happened. Something special and shiny and different had to come to her.

Three big drops, big as tree leaves, slapped his face. Marcos had one idea, two, even three, and maybe four ideas!

Certainly that girl should have been sleeping when he padded into her room. Twilight hush lay softly. A few chirpy insects were at her window. Two birds kept calling each other.

She opened her eyes, seeing Mr. Sweet Potato. "Oh, that's good," she said.

Every day now Grandmomma laughed as she once did. Momma worked in the kitchen, singing while she stirred and baked. Poppa whistled and went back to work.

Marcos knew what was happening. The green rubber tree and fine Mr. Sweet Potato certainly helped. Now Marcia laughed and could even walk around the room, mostly with a limp.

But more needed to be done. Marcia had to feel so fine she could walk without a limp.

On Wednesday he plunked down the shiny old coin on her bed. "Old and valuable," he told her. Even the coin's nicked edges had been smoothed and polished.

On Thursday the strange bottle, blue like the sky, green like grass, found itself on Marcia's bed. The sunshine gleamed through its glass diamonds, making them shine like stars.

Marcos's keen eyes whipped around his room. Mr. Beggar Man had the ice rock, and Grandmomma the golden orchid. The only treasure Marcos had left was the ocean in the pink shell.

Mr. Ocean, noisy and crashing and blue, rested in the pink shell with its rippling folds. Marcos put his ear to the pink shell. He could hear the roar and crash of the waves. Mr. Ocean was in there, trying to get out.

That early evening Marcos helped Poppa stack potatoes on the back porch. Momma sat on the steps shelling peas.

"All Marcia needs now is plenty of fresh air," Poppa said.

"True," said Momma, her eyes troubled. "But we're so far from the beach and the water."

Fresh ocean air! Marcia needed it—air sharp and salty, fresh as blue-green water.

At the beach Marcia could hear the slappy water and feel its tingly wetness. Soft damp air would roll in, making her stronger. She would be as pink and sturdy as a sandcastle!

After a while Marcos sat in Marcia's window, letting the outside darkness cool his back. Marcia wore a lacy robe.

"What if," Marcos asked her, "you had the ocean in your room? Think of all the fine fresh air you would get."

"Silly! You can't bring an ocean into a house!" she said, sounding almost like new. "We'd all drown, and besides, we would get wet and cold and fish would eat us up!"

"That might be so," Marcos said, thinking of all the pesty little fish. But the pink shell carried in its ripply folds sunshine and soppy blue air.

He ran to his room, scooped up the pink shell and came rushing, laughing into her room.

"Here! Just listen!"

Marcia examined the glorious little shell. Its outsides were white; its insides wriggly pink. She held it to her right ear, face glowing. She held it to her left ear, smiling. The funny noisy ocean roared as if it were angry, then crashed as if it were glad.

The waves started from far away, rolling, rushing, crashing hard on the sandy beach. They swept in, bringing wetness and freshness and green seaweed. Marcos and his sister listened, bouncing up and down with their laughing.

Mr. Ocean was there, in Marcia's room!

And Marcia was getting stronger every minute.

Chapter 9

Box Full of Kindness

Blowing rain thrashed down that night. It spattered the windows of Marcos's yellow brick house. It played like soft drums on the red-tiled roof.

Showers drenched the green onions and lettuce and cabbages. Soppy drops washed the fruit trees, soaking the fields. The pond overflowed, making little round rivers in the country road.

Marcos thought Mr. Ocean had escaped from the pink shell.

On that wet splashy morning, Sugar Bread stood on the roof of her shed.

"What," Marcos wondered out loud, "is that ornery goat doing up there?"

Then he heard a sound—"Grrr . . ." A shaggy brown dog growled, barked, and snapped his tail around. He was inviting Sugar Bread to play.

Baby munched on apple cores, paying no attention at all.

Of course nobody ever knew what Sugar Bread might do. So when she jumped to the ground, feet kicking, Marcos yelled, "Run, little dog!"

Just then Sugar Bread sprang into the air. She came down, head lowered, with mean intentions—to butt the poor little dog that just wanted to play. The surprised dog, whipped, ran into the weeds, not coming out again.

"Sugar Bread, you're ornery!" Marcos said, laughing. "You're the funniest little goat in Brazil!" Marcos bounced up and down, imitating the silly goat.

The kitchen smelled good, of sizzling beef and strong onions. It smelled like hot, zingy peppers and juicy black beans and rice.

Marcos didn't expect to see everybody gathered in the sunny kitchen. Poppa and Uncle Antonio sat, strong and able, at the window, sipping black coffee. Grandmomma, wearing a wide apron, stood at the stove. Momma was letting Marcia slice hot yellow bread.

And in the middle of the table, round as the moon, sat a big cake, chocolaty, and on it—candles burning.

"Whose birthday?" Marcos said.

"Yours."

Uncle Antonio winked. Momma said, "On the First of January, we didn't get the chance to celebrate your birthday properly. So we're having another party."

Candles dripped their waxy whiteness onto the chocolate icing. Marcos watched, walking backwards to go wash his hands. Two birthdays would make a fellow twice as old, wouldn't they? And twice as big, wouldn't they?

Everybody waited at the table, Poppa at the head, looking solemn. Momma's face was warm and blushing. Grandmomma and Marcia smiled. Uncle Antonio grinned and asked Marcos to sit next to him.

The candles' little flames glowed bright and happy. Poppa surprised them by saying, "After Marcos blows out his candles, I have something to say."

"Blow, Shorty, blow!" Uncle Antonio said.

Marcos wished and blew, and the smoky candles dripped.

Clearing his throat, Poppa announced, "Gifts of love and kindness are in here." A big box stuck up beside his chair, Grandmomma's yellow robe on top of it.

"Marcos gave these wonderful gifts to his sister while she was sick," Poppa said, smiling, pleased. "I think he saved his treasures a long, long time."

Poppa and Momma were beaming at him. Grandmomma's wrinkled hand folded over Marcos's arm, but Marcia looked a little embarrassed.

Poppa's brown fingers flipped off the the yellow robe so that everybody could see.

Marcos's—or rather—Marcia's special treasures were there.

The shiny green rubber tree in its little red tub sat in the strong palm of Poppa's hand.

"Rich and from the hot country," Grandmother said wisely.

"Why," Momma said, "it has the green of the meadow."

It had known all along how to grow and be happy, sitting in the sun, soaking in the colors, making Marcos proud.

Twitty Mr. Sweet Potato got his share of attention. The clever thing's winding little vines seemed to creep almost everywhere. As for Mr. Sweet Potato, he looked to be winking from one of his potato eyes.

Grandmother insisted that the blue-green bottle, diamonds shining, was the best of the bunch. Uncle Antonio said that the round old coin might bring fortune to Marcos some day.

But Mr. Ocean got the loudest laughs.

"Listen to the roar," said Poppa.

"Listen to the crash," said Marcia.

"I can feel its salty spray," Poppa said.

"Mr. Ocean's fresh wet air helped Marcia get well." Marcos made this announcement, chuckling as he said it.

Everybody clapped.

"Wonderful!" Grandmomma declared.

"Love," Momma said, "and kindness gifts."

That very minute, for some reason, Marcos felt tall. Certainly there was nothing short or low or small about him now. His hand shot up to the curly top of his head. Hey, what was going on up there?

He must have grown a lot.

Everybody at that sugary, syrupy, delicious table smiled at him. A chocolaty cake, waxy drippings on its top, waited to be cut. Marcia was looking at him in the most wonderful way.

It came to Marcos that the secret of growing big did not have so much to do with his height as with his heart.